GOOEY ~~~ EEN,

S

he

'They

and **FU**

LI

# OXFORD
## UNIVERSITY PRESS

Great Clarendon Street, Oxford OX2 6DP
Oxford University Press is a department of the University of Oxford.
It furthers the University's objective of excellence in research, scholarship,
and education by publishing worldwide. Oxford is a registered trade mark
of Oxford University Press in the UK and in certain other countries

British Library Cataloguing in Publication Data

Data available

ISBN: 978-0-19-276375-4

1 3 5 7 9 10 8 6 4 2

Printed in China

Paper used in the production of this book is a natural,
recyclable product made from wood grown in sustainable forests.
The manufacturing process conforms to the environmental
regulations of the country of origin.

DEXTER GREEN · JAKE DASH

# THE GOOZILLAS!

## ESCAPE from the MONSTROUS MAZE

OXFORD
UNIVERSITY PRESS

# WELCOME TO THE
# WORLD OF SLIME

## SIX AWESOME LEVELS TO EXPLORE

Enter a team into the great **GUNGE GAMES**. There are loads of slimy sports to take part in, and win!

Leap from platform to platform, to reach the dizzying heights of the **CRUSTY CRATER**. Whatever you do, don't look down.

It's a fight to the finish line as you speed around this ultimate racing circuit. Can you reach **SLIME CENTRAL** in one piece?

Battle it out in a mission to capture the **FUNGUS FORT**. Beware: you'll need more than ninja skills to defeat the enemies on this level.

Can you escape from the **MONSTROUS MAZE**? Just when you think you're on the right track, the gobbling ghosts will be ready to attack.

Dare you enter the dungeon of slime? Watch your step or you just might end up stuck in the **BOG OF BEASTS**!

# MEET THE GOOZILLAS

## JOE
The joker of the gang. Equipped with special slime-seeking gadget glasses.

## GLOOP
The first Goozilla that Max created, and his favourite by far.

## ATISHOO
A teeny, baby Goozilla, with an enormous sneeze.

## GUNK
A mean, green, fighting machine!

## BIG BLOB
Supersized, and super strong, but definitely not super smart.

## CAPTAIN CRUST
Old, crusty, and in command.

# and the sicklies

## BUBBLE KITTEN

*The evil leader of the Sicklies. She can blow bubble kisses to trap her enemies.*

## SUGAR PAWS PUPPY

*Bubble Kitten's faithful sidekick. His sticky paw prints will stop you in your tracks.*

## GLITTER CHICK

*Watch out for her eggs-plosive glitterbomb eggs.*

## DREAMY BUNNY

*Beware of her powerful hypnotic gaze.*

## SQUEAKY GUINEA PIG

*His supersonic screech will leave your ears ringing.*

## SCAMPY HAMSTER

*The ultimate kickass, street-fighting, rodent.*

# THE STORY SO FAR...

After accidentally **sneezing** all over his tablet computer, Max found himself whisked inside his favourite app, **WORLD OF SLIME**, where he came face-to-face with the Goozillas, a group of green, **slimy** creatures he had created in the game.

When Max discovered that his **sneeze** had destroyed the **GOLDEN GLOB**—a magical artefact that keeps the **WORLD OF SLIME** goo flowing—and that without it the Goozillas' volcano home would completely dry out, he teamed up with his icky new friends and set off to retrieve all the missing pieces, hoping to fix the **GOLDEN GLOB** and bring back the **slime**.

Unfortunately, a group of **cutesy-wootsy**, **sickly-sweet** animals from the neighbouring **World of Pets** app—fed up of having to **dress up** and play on **rainbows** all the time—decided they were going to move in to the **slime** volcano.

If the evil Bubble Kitten and her band of Sicklies get the **GOLDEN GLOB** pieces, then it's the end for the Goozillas, and so thanks to that one fateful **sneeze**, Max has found himself in a frantic race not just to save his new friends, but all of **WORLD OF SLIME** itself!

# CHAPTER ONE

# RETURN TO THE VOLCANO

Max yawned, stretched, opened his eyes, then almost **SCREAMED** when he saw the adorable wide-eyed pink kitten hovering just a few centimetres in front of his face.

'Look what I did to Bubble Kitten,' announced Max's sister, Amy. Her head **POPPED** up above the screen of the tablet and she wore a big grin. Max managed to focus on the screen and saw that the little pink cat was dressed in a puffy yellow dress with a matching hat.

Bubble Kitten was smiling sweetly, but behind the smile there was a look in her eyes that told Max she was secretly furious.

'Aw, that's nice,' said Max, raising his voice and shooting a smile straight back at the on-screen cat. 'She looks like a **FAT BANANA**.'

Amy giggled, then dropped the tablet onto Max's bed. It hit him in the belly, but he didn't complain. Amy never let go of the tablet without a fight, and he was desperate to get back to his Goozillas.

'Mum said I have to give it to you,' Amy explained. 'We're going to the shops because you've used up all the tissues in the house and we have to get some more.'

Max sat up and wiped his **rußßy ßose** on his duvet. The duvet cover was green and **WORLD OF SLIME** themed, so he didn't think anyone would notice.

'How you feeling, Maxy?' called Mum from downstairs.

'Rubbish!' Max croaked, and he wasn't lying. His cold wasn't going away. If anything, it was getting worse. His head felt like a waterbomb filled with **snot**.

Max smiled. He'd never been happier to be ill in all his life.

'We'll only be an hour or so,' promised

Mum. 'I'll make you breakfast when we get back. You stay in bed for now.'

'OK!' said Max. There was a tingling at the back of his nose that told him a **sneeze** was coming. Quickly, he shut down the World of Pets app and tapped on the  icon.

The app opened, revealing the **slimy** volcano that made up the main part of the game. A group of green **splodges** stood on the ground floor of the volcano. Max quickly tapped the shop icon, then scrolled to the list of vehicles. If he and the Goozillas were going to go in search of the rest of the pieces of the **GOLDEN GLOB**, they'd need a way to get around.

'**AHA!**' Max cried out loud. He'd found

the perfect thing. Without a moment's hesitation, he **HIT** the buy button and watched as a few hundred dung dollars left his account.

'You'd better go, Amy,' said Max, turning to his sister. His nostrils had begun to twitch. 'Mum's waiting.'

On the screen, the Goozillas turned to watch in **WONDER** as a large wooden crate was delivered to them.

'Aw, can't I just hang out with you for a while?' Amy asked, flopping onto the bed by his feet.

'**NO!**' said Max, urgently. The sneeze was building quickly now. He could feel his eyes starting to water. 'You need to go. **NOW!**'

'Aw, but . . .'

'**COME ON, AMY!**' Mum shouted up the stairs.

'See?' said Max in a breathless whisper. There was a full-scale **bogey blast** building behind his **nose**, but he didn't dare **UNLEASH** it while his sister was there.

Amy tutted and got up. 'Fine,' she said. 'But I'm playing **World of Pets** when I get back. I've made a new pet and she needs—'

'**JUST G-GO!**' Max urged. His eyes

screwed shut just as Amy headed for the
door. His head snapped back, his mouth
opening wide.

# ATCHOO!

'Bless you,' called Amy
from halfway down the stairs.
'Thanks,' Max replied. At least, he started to
reply, but as his **snot** splattered across
the tablet's screen, his bedroom twisted and
twirled around him. Just like last time, a
strange feeling wobbled through him, like
he was being turned inside out and upside-

down and back-to-front.

The bed vanished. The room, too. There was a loud **SPLINTERING** sound, like breaking wood, as Max landed on top of a big wooden crate.

The four walls of the box fell outwards, one by one, and Max found himself sitting on a broken plank, on top of a green and yellow vehicle that looked like a cross between a camper van and a tank. Or was it more like a Monster Truck crossed with a school bus? Max couldn't make his mind up.

On the ground below, a group of **slimy** green **blobs** looked up at him and gasped.

'Hey guys, I came back!' said Max, waving down at the Goozillas. 'And I bought you a Bogey Bus!'

# CHAPTER TWO

# ALL ABOARD!

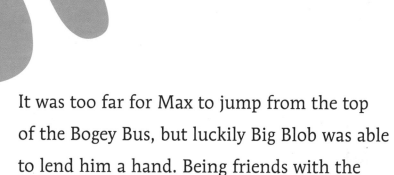

It was too far for Max to jump from the top of the Bogey Bus, but luckily Big Blob was able to lend him a hand. Being friends with the **BIGGEST** and **STRONGEST** Goozilla who had ever lived certainly came in handy, sometimes.

'What a marvellous gift,' said Captain Crust, giving Max a salute as Big Blob set him safely on the ground. 'Thank you, Max.'

'It's **AWESOME!**' cried Joe, scanning the vehicle with his high-tech Gadget Glasses. 'Can I drive it?'

Gunk, the gruffest and grumpiest Goozilla, spun his *SLUDGESPUTTER 6000* slime gun on one **gooey** finger and snorted. 'No way! You're far too young.'

'Then perhaps I should be the driver?' Captain Crust suggested.

'You're far too old,' said Gunk.

Atishoo, the tiniest Goozilla  of all, opened his mouth, but Gunk interrupted before he'd even started to speak. 'And you're too small to reach the pedals. I'll be the driver.'

Max let out a little **YELP** of surprise as a pair of **squidgy** arms wrapped around him and hugged him tightly from behind. He looked round to see his first ever Goozilla, Gloop, grinning back at him. 'Good to have you back, Max!'

'It's good to be back,' Max smiled. There

was a **slurp** sound as Gloop unwrapped his **jelly-like** arms from around Max and stepped back.

'The Bogey Bus is amazing!' he said. 'It'll make getting around much easier.'

'We'll need it, too,' said Captain Crust, and he motioned around them. Max could see that the volcano's **slime** was even crustier-looking than the last time he was here. 'We must gather the remaining parts of the **GOLDEN GLOB**,' the Captain continued, 'so it can bring back the **slime**, or our world is doomed.'

'Then what are we waiting for?' cried Joe.

'ALL ABOARD THE BOGEY BUS!'

The top part of the Bogey Bus, where the driver and passengers went, was **CHUNKY** and rectangular, with rows of seats lined up inside. Where the wheels should have been, though, were **ENORMOUS** caterpillar tracks—just the thing for travelling on roads made of **goo** and **slime**.

As one, the Goozillas *RACED* for the bus's ladder, falling over one another as they hurried to climb on.

'**TALLY-HO!**' cried Captain Crust.

'**WATCH IT!**' snapped Gunk.

'**SMALLEST FIRST!**' insisted Atishoo.

'**COMING THROUGH!**' warned Joe.

'**SQUASH UP, EVERYONE!**' said Gloop.

They all tumbled into the Bogey Bus, then stopped. The inside of the bus was tired and worn, with stains on the floor and rips on the seats. The steering wheel had broken off at some point, and had been repaired using tape.

'Well, this is . . . nice,' said Captain Crust.

'Uh, yeah,' said Max, blushing a little at the bottom step. 'It's second-hand. I didn't have enough Dung Dollars for a new one.'

'**ROOM FOR ONE MORE?**' boomed Big Blob, squeezing inside. The other Goozillas all **GASPED** as they were flattened against the windows by Big Blob's blobby bigness.

'Well dis is comfortable,' mumbled Joe, his face **squashed** against the glass. Big Blob

**17**

**ooᶻed** his way to the back of the bus, and there followed a loud **SCREECHING** sound as his head pushed upwards and made a hole through the metal roof.

'That's better,' he said. And so, with half of Big Blob sticking out of the bus, there was just room for Max to hop aboard. He jumped into the chair next to Gloop, but just as his bum touched the seat, an **enormous fart** echoed around the bus. Everyone turned to Max, looking shocked. He blushed.

**'THAT WASN'T ME!'** he cried, as he reached under his bum and pulled out a flat whoopee cushion.

'Sorry,' Joe giggled. Max had based Goozilla Joe on his real-life best friend, Joe. Like the real Joe, the Goozilla version loved to play practical jokes. 'Couldn't resist.'

Gunk **FLOORED** the accelerator pedal and the Bogey Bus's caterpillar tracks spun, tossing flakes of dried-out **slime** into the air behind them.

'Here goes!' said Gunk, and the bus **SHOT** forwards. Everyone cheered as they **BOUNCED** and **TRUNDLED** across the rocky ground, heading straight towards a circle of light in the shadows up ahead.

'So where are we going?' asked Max.

'Where's the next part of the **GOLDEN GLOB**?'

'It's on level two,' Joe explained. 'I tracked

it with my Gadget Glasses.'

'Level two?' said Max. The

**WORLD OF SLIME** volcano was made up

of six different levels, each one with its own

theme. The level they were driving through

now was the dungeon. Max knew only too

well what waited for them on the next level.

'That's the **MONSTROUS MAZE**!'

Before anyone could answer, the Bogey

Bus *SHOT* through the hole in the side of

the volcano and *ROARED* out into the

world beyond. Max blinked in the sudden

brightness, then clapped his hand over his

mouth to stop himself **SCREAMING** at the

sight before him. The bus was *THUNDERING*

up a narrow road with the volcano, right next

to the bus, on one side. And on the other side,

21

just a few centimetres from the bus's tracks, was a sheer drop down into a **bubbling** pit of dark green **sludge**.

One wrong move from Gunk, and they'd all be **DOOMED**!

'Steady as she goes, Gunk,' said Captain Crust.

'**I KNOW WHAT I'M DOING, BUB**,' Gunk grunted in reply.

Max turned away from the window, too scared to keep looking. 'So, the **GLOB** piece is in the maze?' he said, shakily. 'Will the maze's bad guys be there? Those **gooey** ghosts?'

'The Gools,' said Joe, shuddering. 'Yep.'

'But we'll get past them. You've played the maze level before, haven't you, Max?' said Gloop.

Max nodded. 'Played it? Yes,' he said. He swallowed nervously. 'Escaped it? No.'

# CHAPTER THREE

# INTO THE MAZE

The Bogey Bus turned sharply to the left, throwing everyone around in their seats. Atishoo boinged around like a rubber ball, bouncing off the windows, before finally landing with a faint **SPLAT** on Captain Crust's hat.

Max looked out of the window just as the bus *SKIDDED* back inside the volcano through a hole in its side. It was like being on a train going into a tunnel, and Max was just starting to get used to the darkness when he spotted some bright lights twinkling up ahead.

'What's that?' he wondered.

'That, my dear boy,' Captain Crust whispered, 'is the **MONSTROUS MAZE**!'

With its neon lights, the **MONSTROUS MAZE** was the most futuristic-looking of all the levels in **WORLD OF SLIME**. The point of the game was to make your way through a twisting maze, collecting **power-ups**, and dodging ghosts. If you made it to the middle of the maze, you won. If the ghosts caught you, it was game over.

The first few mazes were easy, and Max could find his way to the centre with his eyes closed. Later stages were much more difficult, though. There were ten different mazes in total, and while Max could get round most of them, he'd never made it through the final stage, **THE LUMPY LABYRINTH**, without being gobbled by ghosts.

The Bogey Bus stopped near the entrance of the first maze. The doors opened. 'Right, you lot. Off you get,' Gunk announced. Max, Gloop, and Joe *RACED* for the door and jumped out.

'**WHOA!**' said Gloop, gazing admiringly at the maze walls. 'I'd forgotten how cool it looks.' The walls themselves were black, but with bright stripes of colourful light running along them. Every few seconds, a much brighter light would *SHOOT* along the stripes, making it look as if something was *WHIZZING* around the maze at super speed.

'There's no **slime** here,' Max realized, as a horrible thought struck him. 'Has it all dried up? Are we too late?'

'There is **slime**,' said Atishoo in his tiny voice. 'It's over there, look.'

Having no arms made it a bit difficult to point, so Atishoo nodded his head, instead. Max looked in the direction of the nod and saw hundreds of **little green squares** dotted around the top of the maze.

'It's **pixel slime**,' explained Gloop. 'Instead of a big splodge of **slime**, it's lots of **little slime squares** all gathered together.'

'It's **STYLISH**, apparently,' said Gunk, shuddering at the word. 'Don't see it, myself.' He waved his gun towards the maze entrance. 'So, the **GLOB** piece is in there?'

Joe switched on his Gadget Glasses scanner and studied the maze. 'Yep! Looks like it's right in the middle.'

Captain Crust stroked his moustache thoughtfully. 'How in the name of all that is **oo²y** are we supposed to find the centre?'

'Easy. This is the level one maze,' said Max, striding towards the entrance. 'I'll get us there in no time.'

Max led the others into the maze and strolled casually down the first long, straight corridor, feeling relaxed and confident.

'What about the ghosts?' whispered Gloop, his big eyes darting left and right.

'Don't worry. They don't show up until level two,' Max reassured him. He took a right turn, then an immediate left. 'There's nothing dangerous in the first maze.'

The slow-moving Captain Crust had fallen

behind, so they stopped to let him catch up. The captain was the oldest Goozilla, but boasted some impressive military training, and an even more impressive moustache. He might not be **QUICK**, but his army skills could come in useful.

Once the group was together again, it took Max less than a minute to lead them to the centre of the maze.

And there, floating in the air ahead of them, was a piece of the **GOLDEN GLOB**!

'Well, that was easy,' said Big Blob.

'Indeed,' agreed Captain Crust, wheezing slightly. 'Mission accomplished.'

'I'll get it,' said Gloop, **oozing**
across the floor. But when he reached out
to collect the **GLOB** piece, his hands passed
straight through it. 'Huh?' he said. He tried
again, but the result was the same.

'It's a hologram,' said Joe, studying the
chunk of **GOLDEN GLOB** through his glasses.
'It's not really there. It's a trick.'

'Are you sure?' asked Captain Crust.

'I'm the king of practical jokes,' said Joe. 'I
know a trick when I see one.'

Captain Crust raised his walking stick and
took aim at nothing in particular. Although it
looked just like a regular stick, it was secretly
a **slime-shooting** weapon. 'I fear this may
be a trap,' he whispered, glancing about him.

'Oh, put that useless piece of junk away,'

said Gunk, raising his own gun. 'Let a real soldier handle this.'

'I don't get it,' squeaked Atishoo. 'Why would someone try to lead us here?'

But before anyone could answer, something pink and glittery rolled into the centre of the maze and stopped at Big Blob's feet. It was the size of a bowling ball, but not quite the same shape.

'Hey,' said Big Blob. 'It's an egg.'

And then, with a **BOOM**, the egg exploded.

# CHAPTER FOUR

# THE NEW CHICK

The **BLAST** from the **EGG-BOMB** hit Big Blob full in the face, covering him in sparkly pink glitter. The force of the explosion would have knocked the other Goozillas off their feet, but luckily Big Blob was made from **STRONGER** stuff.

'Heh,' he said, blinking slowly. 'That tickled.'

'What was that?' cried Gloop, coughing in the cloud of glittering sparkles.

'Why, it was an **EGG-SPLOSION**, of course,' purred an all-too-familiar voice.

Max and the Goozillas spun round to see

the pink, wide-eyed face of a kitten glaring at them through the glitter-dust. 'Bubble Kitten!' Max yelped. 'I should have guessed.'

'**IT'S SLIME TIME, BUB!**' roared Gunk. He opened fire on the cat, spraying her with a stream of sticky **gloop** from his *SLUDGESPUTTER*.

Bubble Kitten sniggered as the **slime** passed harmlessly through her. 'She's a hologram, too!' Max realized.

The kitten's head floated into the air, growing larger until it almost filled the whole centre of the maze.

'Well done. You're smarter than you look,' she said. 'Although, to be fair, you do look *incredibly* dumb.'

'Hey, Bubble Kitten, where's the banana costume my sister dressed you in earlier?' Max taunted. 'It really suited you.'

'It made me look like an idiot,' Bubble Kitten hissed.

'Exactly,' Max grinned. 'Like I said, it really suited you.'

'**GOOD ONE, MAX**,' said Gloop. He and Max exchanged a fist bump, while Captain Crust shuffled forward.

'What have you done with the **GOLDEN**

**GLOB**?' he demanded.

'Oh, I wouldn't worry about that,' sneered Bubble Kitten. 'You've got bigger problems. Like finding your way out of the maze, for one.'

'Easy,' said Max. 'This is the level one maze. I could get us out of here in thirty seconds.'

'**EGG-CELLENT POINT**,' said Bubble Kitten, her green eyes flashing with **EXCITEMENT**. 'Let's **EGGS-CHANGE** it for something more challenging, shall we?'

Max and the Goozillas all **JUMPED** in fright as the walls around them began to move. From all across the maze came the sounds of groaning and grinding. The maze was changing shape around them!

'Let's try level seven,' Bubble Kitten

sniggered. 'This one looks **EGG-CITING**.'

Gloop and Joe both swallowed nervously and drew closer to Max. 'This one has ghosts, right?' Gloop whispered.

'Yeah,' croaked Max. 'This one has ghosts.'

'And that's not all!' cried Bubble Kitten's floating head. 'Behold, the latest addition to my pet army. Turn and look into the true face of evil!'

Max and the others spun round to find a small yellow bird standing behind them, gazing up. It had a tiny red bow in its hair, and the longest eyelashes Max had ever seen.

'**GLITTER CHICK!**' Bubble Kitten boomed.

'**ALRIGHT?**' said Glitter Chick in a surprisingly deep voice.

**40**

# ATC

A powerful sneeze shot Atishoo backwards off Captain Crust's hat. He bounced off a wall, rebounded off another, then went **SPLAT** on the ground. 'Sorry,' he mumbled. 'I'm allergic to feathers.'

They all turned back to Glitter Chick, but the little bird was gone. In her place was an egg almost as **BIG** as she was. This one was green with blue sparkles. From inside it,

Max could hear a tick-tick-ticking sound.

'Have fun, everyone,' said Bubble Kitten's big floating head. 'But I should warn you, that last egg was just a warm up. This one is **EGGS-TRA EGG-SPLOSIVE!**'

The kitten's laughter echoed all across the maze. 'If I were you, I'd start running!'

# CHAPTER FIVE

# THE GHOSTLY GOOLS

There was no time to lose! Max and the Goozillas took off at a *RUN*, trying to put as much distance between themselves and the **EGG-BOMB** as possible. They *DUCKED* around a corner just as the egg **EXPLODED** with an **ENORMOUS BANG** that shook the whole maze.

Once they were sure it was safe, Max and Gloop carefully peeked out. The whole centre of the maze was a smoking crater of sparkly glitter. The hologram of the **GOLDEN GLOB** fizzled and flickered for a moment, then vanished.

'Phew, that was close,' said Gloop and Max. When Max had created Gloop, he'd given him all the same personality traits as Max himself had, which meant they often thought the same thing at the same time. '**JINX!**' they said together. '**JINX AGAIN!**'

'**THIS IS NO TIME FOR GAMES!**' Gunk growled. 'We have to find our way out.'

'Any idea which route to follow, Max?' asked Captain Crust, his dry old body creaking as he turned to study the exits. Atishoo had clambered back on top of his hat again, where he could

keep a look-out for danger.

There were six different corridors leading away from them. Max peered along them, trying to work out where they were. 'It looks familiar,' he mumbled, gazing up at the tall walls with their flashy lights and **pixel slime**. 'I think . . . we've gone towards the north-east corner of the maze,' he said.

Then his eyes went **WIDE** and his jaw **DROPPED** in realization. '**OH NO!**'

'Please tell me you meant that in a good way,' said Joe.

'Why would he gasp and say "oh no," in a good way?' grunted Gunk.

'I don't know!' Joe said. 'Maybe where he comes from it's a good thing. Like, "Oh no, I've just been given a lovely big cake," or, "Oh no, I've just won a zillion dung dollars," or something.'

'No, it's n-nothing good,' stammered Max. He dropped his voice. 'We're near the Gool base.'

'Those ghost chaps?' Captain Crust whispered. 'Pah! Back in my day . . .'

Gunk groaned. '**UGH**. Give me Gools over one of his stories *any* day!'

'Um, I think you're in luck, Gunk,' said Atishoo. He ducked low on Captain Crust's hat. 'Look!'

Gunk and the others all followed Atishoo's gaze. They **GASPED** in fright at what they saw. Floating towards them, its square eyes fixed on them, was an **ENORMOUS** red ghost!

**'LEAVE THIS TO ME!'** said Gunk, taking aim with his gun. He launched a stream of sticky **sludge** at the ghost. 'A blast of the **SLUDGESPUTTER** will stop that thing in its tracks.' The **slime** struck the ghost right in its belly, but instead of sticking, the **goo** slid harmlessly off.

'Well, that was a complete waste of time,' said Joe.

'You can't shoot them,' said Max. 'You can only destroy them if you've eaten a **Power-Up Fruit**.'

'And do we have any?' asked Captain Crust.

'**NO!**' Max yelped.

'Ah. Right,' said Captain Crust. 'Then I

suggest we run for it!'

And with that, they all turned towards one of the other corridors, only to find a pale blue ghost drifting along it in their direction.

'**DOWN THERE!**'

urged Gunk.

But this time, when they turned, they saw a sparkly yellow bird hopping towards them. Glitter Chick!

ATC

Atishoo sneezed and shot straight into Max's arms. 'Sorry,' Atishoo said. 'Feathers.'

'**THIS WAY!**' cried Max, turning and heading for the corridor on his left.

'**THIS WAY!**' said Gloop at exactly the same time, heading for the corridor on his right.

Holding tightly to Atishoo, Max stumbled around a corner and *THREW* himself into a run. He *DODGED* and *WEAVED* around a series of sharp turns, then stopped to catch his breath.

HOO!

'Everyone . . . OK?' he panted. He turned and saw Big Blob staring blankly at him. Max leaned around the giant Goozilla. 'Gloop? Joe? Are you—' he began, but then stopped.

Max stared at the empty corridor behind Big Blob. There was no Gloop, no Joe, no anyone.

The other Goozillas were **GONE**.

# CHAPTER SIX

# SPLIT-UP

## 'GLOOP! JOE! WHERE ARE YOU?'

Max shouted. His voice rolled in both directions along the corridor, echoing off the walls.

'Shh!' urged Atishoo. 'The Gools will hear you.'

'We have to go back,' said Max. 'What if they've been caught? What if they're in trouble?'

A pink face appeared in the air in front of them, shimmering slightly. The Bubble Kitten hologram grinned down at Max. 'Aw, look at you. So worried about your slimy little friends. How sickening.'

'The only sickly thing around here is you, Bubble Kitten!' said Max. 'Where are they?'

'I have them,' Bubble Kitten replied, triumphantly. 'They are all my prisoners.'

'What?' said a voice from somewhere behind Bubble Kitten's head. 'Since when?'

A furry blue face squeezed into the hologram alongside the cat, nudging her out of the way. Max recognized Bubble Kitten's faithful sidekick, Sugar Paws Puppy, straight away.

Sugar Paws gazed at Max and the others, his tongue hanging out. 'Oh look, it's them green things and that boy from last time. **HIYA!**' he called, waving a big shaggy paw. 'Nice to see you all again.'

'**WILL YOU *SHUT UP?***'

hissed Bubble Kitten, shoving Sugar Paws. 'And yes, I *do* have the others held prisoner, actually.'

'Do you?' asked Sugar Paws. His hologram turned, looking around. 'Where are they?'

'They're in . . . er . . . my prison,' stuttered Bubble Kitten.

Sugar Paws frowned. 'Since when did you have a prison? Are you sure you're not making this up?'

**'NO! OF COURSE I'M NOT MAKING IT UP!'** Bubble Kitten snapped. 'I *definitely* have them locked up in my prison, OK?'

called Gloop's voice from somewhere in the maze. 'We must have got separated. Don't worry, though, we're all safe. We haven't been taken prisoner or anything.'

'Are you *sure* you're holding them prisoner?' said Sugar Paws. 'It's just, that voice sounded a lot like—'

'**FINE!** OK, I *don't* have them prisoner, alright? Happy now?' Bubble Kitten sighed and shook her head, before turning her attention back to Max. 'It doesn't matter. You'll never find your way out of here. And you'll never get your hands on this.'

The hologram held up a shiny shard of **GOLD**.

'The **GLOB**!' Max gasped.

'The **GLOB**!' Atishoo squeaked.

'Hey, look, a pink cat,' said Big Blob, slowly. Not for the first time, Max thought he should probably have given Big Blob more brainpower points.

'You won't get away with this, Bubble Kitten,' Max warned.

'Oh, my dear boy,' the cat purred. 'I already have. Enjoy the maze. And do say hello to Glitter Chick for me. I'm sure she's somewhere close by.'

And with that, the hologram faded, leaving behind only the echo of Bubble Kitten's laughter.

'That cat has some *serious* issues,' Atishoo sighed. 'We need to get that piece of the **GOLDEN GLOB**.'

'And we need to get out of here,' replied Max.

'And we need to find our friends,' said Big Blob.

Max looked up at the giant Goozilla and nodded. 'You're right, Blob. That's our first mission. We need to find the others.' He looked up at the tall walls towering around them. 'And I know just how we can do it!'

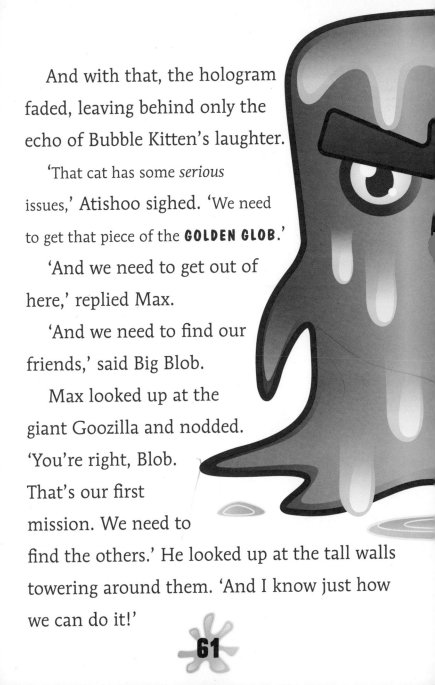

# CHAPTER SEVEN

# MAX THE NAVIGATOR

A few minutes later, Max wobbled unsteadily on Big Blob's head. His feet were ankle deep in sludgy, **slimy goo**, and he felt like he might sink further at any moment. He hoped not, because if he sunk any deeper, he'd end up inside the Goozilla's tummy.

Beneath Max, Big Blob shuffled closer to the wall. Max bent his knees and held one arm out, trying to keep his balance. 'Steady . . . Steady . . .'

Even standing on Big Blob's head, Max wasn't tall enough to see over the wall. But luckily, he didn't have to be. Carefully raising

himself up, Max stretched both arms above him as high as they would go. In his hands, Atishoo let out a little **CHEER**.

'**I CAN SEE OVER THE WALL!**' the little Goozilla announced.

'Brilliant!' said Max. 'What can you see?'

'Um . . . more maze,' said Atishoo. 'That's all.'

Max nodded. He'd been expecting that answer. 'OK, here goes,' he whispered, then he raised his voice into a

# LOUD SHOUT.

# 'GUNK! SHOOT YOUR GUN INTO THE AIR.'

They all listened to Max's voice echo away. At first, Max thought Gunk hadn't heard, and he was just getting ready to shout again when he heard the splurt of **SLUDGESPUTTER** fire.

'I see it! I see it!' cried Atishoo. 'They're in a z-shaped bend that goes left at one end and right at the other.'

Max closed his eyes and tried to picture the maze. Level seven was tricky, but he'd mastered it after many hours of practice. If he concentrated, he could see the whole maze as if he were

looking down on it from

above, just like when he

played the game on his tablet.

'OK, I know where you are, guys. **WAIT RIGHT THERE!**' he called. And he slid down Big Blob's back then set off **RUNNING**, Atishoo still clutched in his arms. Big Blob did his best to keep up, but he was built for **STRENGTH**, not **SPEED**, so Max had to stop a few times to let him catch up.

After a few minutes of **RUNNING**, Max **SKIDDED** around another bend. 'It's just right, left, two more rights, and we should see them,' he announced.

He raced around the first right, then

**YELPED** and **DUCKED** as a sparkly yellow egg came sailing towards him.

'**SURPRISE!**' boomed Glitter Chick, just as the wall behind Max erupted in an explosion of colourful sprinkles. The feathery fiend took aim with another egg, and Max frantically retreated.

'**GET BACK!**' he warned Big Blob. He tucked Atishoo under his arm and *RAN* towards Big Blob, just as the second egg-bomb detonated behind him. The **FORCE** of the **BLAST** *LAUNCHED* Max through the air in a cloud of smoke and sparkles.

He hit Big Blob in the centre of the chest with a squelchy **SPLAT**. Wrapping his arms around Max, Big Blob turned and *RAN*, chased by the echo of Glitter Chick's deep, rumbling laughter.

'**BIG BLOB WILL KEEP MAX SAFE!**' growled the enormous Goozilla, weaving his way through turn after turn, taking them deeper and deeper into the maze.

'Blob, wait!' cried Max. 'We can stop

**69**

now. I don't think Glitter Chick is chasing us anymore.'

Big Blob stumbled on for a few more paces, then stopped. 'Where are we?' he asked.

'No idea,' said Max. 'Ready to be lookout again, Atishoo?'

'You bet!'

Scrambling back onto Big Blob's head, Max stretched up, holding Atishoo as high as he could.

The little Goozilla peeked over the wall, then let out a **YELP** of fright when he spotted a face peering back at him.

'**WAH!**' wailed Atishoo.

'**WAH!**' replied the face.

'Hey, is that Joe?' asked Max.

It was! Joe was on the other side of the wall, balancing on a tower of Goozillas!

'**HEY, MAX!**' he shouted.

'**HI, MAX!**' added Gloop, sounding a little further away.

'Can we *please* hurry this up?' demanded Gunk. His voice was low and muffled, and Max guessed he must be at the bottom of the pile.

'Wait there!' said Max. 'We'll be right with you.'

Jumping down, Max *RACED* around a couple

of bends, just in time to see the tower of Goozillas **COLLAPSE** on top of Gunk. They all quickly jumped up again, grinning excitedly.

'Max, you found us!' said Gloop.

'You're a genius!' said Joe.

'**OW**,' said Gunk.

'Look what we found,' said Joe.

Plunging a hand inside his tummy, Joe rummaged around. Max watched in wonder. He didn't think he'd ever get used to seeing the Goozillas reach inside themselves like that, but he had to admit it was a pretty handy way of storing stuff.

Joe pulled out a pair of roller skates. 'No, not that,' he said, tossing the skates over his shoulder. He reached into his belly several more times, pulling out some plastic dog poo, a catapult, and a rubber chicken.

'**OH, HURRY UP!**' snapped Gunk, his eyes searching the corridor for danger.

# 'HERE THEY ARE!'
Joe announced.

He held out a small bunch of cherries. Max bent down and studied them. They didn't look like real cherries, but were instead made up of **pixels**, just like the **slime**. He recognized them right away.

'That's **Power—Up Fruit**,' Max said.

'Five of them!' laughed Gloop. 'They'll come in handy if we meet the Gools again.'

Captain Crust shuffled up to Max and smiled beneath his moustache. 'Now, young Max, we need to track down those **Sicklies** and get back the **GLOB** piece. Am I correct in thinking you know how to find the way out?'

'I do!' said Max, turning in the direction of another corridor. But before he could take a step, an **ENORMOUS** floating head appeared in the air.

'**GLITTER CHICK!**' Max growled.

'The one and only,' the villain clucked. 'Did you enjoy those eggs I laid for you? I thought they were the bomb.' Her beak curved into a wicked grin. 'I hope they didn't make you even more lost.'

'Ha! We're not lost,' said Max. 'I know my way around this maze like the back of my hand!'

'**OH, REALLY?**' purred Bubble Kitten, her head appearing in the air beside Glitter Chick's. 'We'll have to see about that, won't we?'

'Too right,' agreed Glitter Chick, gruffly.

She and Bubble Kitten both laughed as the walls around the Goozillas began to move once more. They **DOUBLED** in height, causing an eerie shadow to fall over the Goozillas, then twisted and turned until they'd formed an entirely new set of corridors. The floor lit up in a sinister shade of red. 'Let's see how you cope with level ten,' clucked Glitter Chick, a smirk tugging at the corners of her beak.

'Behold!' cried Bubble Kitten, triumphantly. **'THE LUMPY LABYRINTH**!'
**'OF DOOOOOOM!**' added Sugar Paws from behind her.

Bubble Kitten sighed and rolled her wide green eyes. 'No, it's just **THE LUMPY LABYRINTH**.'

'What?' said Sugar Paws, squeezing his way into the hologram between Bubble Kitten and Glitter Chick. 'It's not **THE LUMPY**

**LABYRINTH OF DOOM**? Why not? That sounds much better.'

'It does sound better,' Glitter Chick agreed.

**'OH, DON'T YOU START**,' Bubble Kitten snapped. The holograms all vanished.

Then reappeared again.

**'SO LONG, LOSERS!'** spat Glitter Chick. The image faded and this time didn't return.

Captain Crust tucked his cane beneath his arm. 'Well then, Max. Lead the way!'

Max shook his head. 'I . . . I can't,' he said. 'I've never beaten **THE LUMPY LABYRINTH** before.'

He took a deep breath and looked across the faces of his friends. 'No one ever has!'

# CHAPTER EIGHT

# SNOT TO BE SNIFFED AT

Joe peered through his Gadget Glasses.
'I've got good news and bad news,' he
announced. 'The bad news is, I can't see
anything that might help us find the way
out.'

'What's the good news?' asked Max.

Joe shrugged. 'Um, I don't know. It's not
raining. Nobody is on fire. Those are pretty
good.'

'We should just pick a direction and
start walking,' Gunk grunted. He punched
a fist in the air and raised his voice.
**'RIGHT! WHO'S WITH ME?'**

No one moved. Gunk tutted. 'Fine. Suit yourselves.'

'We can't just go wandering off,' Max explained. 'We'll just get ourselves more lost.'

'But we can't just stay here, either,' said Gloop.

Captain Crust's head made a sound like dried out old **bogies** as he nodded. 'Gloop

**80**

is correct. We must find our way out and get
the piece of the **GOLDEN GLOB** before it is
too late.'

Max looked at Joe's belly. 'Don't suppose
you've got a sniffer dog in there, have you?'

'Not that I've noticed,' said Joe.

'Pity,' Max sighed. 'Because we could use
its **nose** to track down . . .'

Max froze, his eyes wide.

'Max?' said Gloop. He waved a hand in front of Max's face, but Max didn't blink. Instead, an **EXCITED SMILE** spread across his face.

'We don't have a sniffer dog, but there is a **nose** we can use!' Max cried. Atishoo giggled as Max thrust him into the air. 'Atishoo can help us track down Bubble Kitten so we can get the **GLOB** piece back.'

'How did she even get the **GLOB** piece, anyway?' Joe wondered.

'I don't know,' admitted Max. 'Maybe Sugar Paws is a tracker dog, and sniffed it out.'

'But Atishoo isn't. How can he sniff out Bubble Kitten?' asked Gunk.

'Because Bubble Kitten is with Glitter Chick!'

**82**

Everyone blinked. 'So?'

'*So*, Glitter Chick is covered in feathers.'

'And Atishoo is allergic to feathers!' Gloop gasped. **'THAT'S GENIUS!'**

Max held Atishoo out in front of him with both hands. 'Tell me if your nose tickles,' he said, slowly turning on the spot.

'Well, I don't actually have a nose,' Atishoo pointed out. 'But I'll do my best.'

He closed his eyes as Max pointed him towards three different corridors. 'Anything?' Max asked.

'No, not really,' Atishoo said. 'Wait! Back one!'

Max turned back to one of the corridors. Atishoo twitched his face as he felt a tingling. 'That way!'

'You sure?' asked Max.

Atishoo let rip with a **Snot-Spraying Sneeze**. Max was thrown backwards against the wall by the **FORCE** of it. Atishoo grinned.

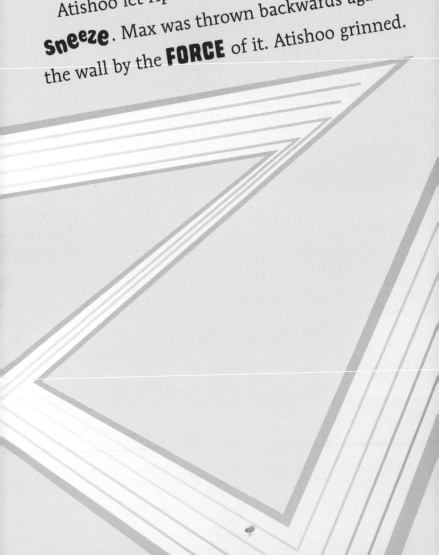

# 'PRETTY SURE!'

They made their way through the maze,
following Atishoo's nose.

At every junction they stopped and waited for a **sneeze** to build, then *HURRIED* in that direction.

'This is never going to work,' Gunk muttered after ten minutes of **sneeze-searching**.

'You were saying?' Max whispered, pointing along the corridor ahead of them. There, heading for the exit, were Bubble Kitten, Sugar Paws Puppy, and Glitter Chick. Max patted Atishoo on his **slime-coated** head. 'Better than a Sat Nav!' he said.

'And there's the **GLOB** piece!' said Gloop. Sure enough, the **GOLDEN SHARD** was clutched in Bubble Kitten's front paws. If they didn't stop her soon, Bubble Kitten would take it right back to the *World of*

Pets, and the **WORLD OF SLIME** would be doomed forever.

'**WHAT DO WE DO NOW?**' Joe wondered, a little too loudly.

'Allow me to answer that,' said Bubble Kitten, turning to face the Goozillas. She and Glitter Chick both grinned wickedly. Sugar Paws *CHASED* his tail for a second, then tried to sniff his own bottom. 'I suspected you might track us down somehow. Well done. It will, however, be the last thing you ever do. Gools . . . **ATTACK!**'

Max and the Goozillas **GROANED** as six colourful ghosts emerged from corridors all around them and began to close in.

'TA-TA, GOO-ZEROES,'

Bubble Kitten said.

'SEE YA,'

Glitter Chick added, in her deep, booming voice.

'WOULDN'T WANNA BE YA.'

Big Blob pushed past Max and moved to block the Gools. 'Big Blob will handle this,' he said, drawing back a fist.

## 'WAIT, BLOB, DON'T!'

Max yelped. 'You can't fight them. You can't even touch them!'

'Why ever not?' asked Captain Crust.

'Because if we touch them, we'll become Gools ourselves,' Max explained. 'And we'll be trapped in the maze

## FOREVER!'

# CHAPTER NINE

# GOOLS VS. GOOZILLAS

Max and the others watched, helplessly, as the Sicklies **RACED** out of the maze with the **GLOB** piece. The ghostly Gools were closing in on the Goozillas . . . and fast. There was **NOWHERE** to *RUN*.

'**WAIT! THE CHERRIES!**' exclaimed Max.

'Yeah, we may as well have something to eat if we're going to be stuck here,' said Gunk.

'No, they're **Power—Up Fruit**!' Max replied. 'They'll stop us being turned into Gools. We'll be able to fight them!'

'**OF COURSE!**' cried Joe, and he pressed

a hand against Max's belly. Max frowned.

'What are you doing?'

'Getting the cherries out of your guts,' said Joe.

Max reached into his pocket and took out the cherries. 'I use pockets to carry stuff around.'

'**EW**,' said Joe, wrinkling his face up. 'That's just weird.'

Max counted out the fruit. 'Five cherries, seven of us,' he said. 'There aren't enough.'

'Don't you worry about me,' said Captain Crust. 'I'll be fine without one. Why, back in my day . . .'

He stopped talking when a cherry was **FLICKED** into his mouth. Max took aim and **FIRED** the other four. Gloop, Big Blob, Joe, and Gunk all caught them in their mouths and swallowed.

Their green bodies began to **GLOW** and everyone—even the already **MASSIVE** Blob—seemed to grow a little.

'Now you'll be able to touch the Gools without getting hurt,' Max explained. 'But you'll have to destroy them quickly, before it wears off.'

'But what about you and Atishoo?' Gloop asked.

'You five deal with the Gools,' Max said, tucking Atishoo under one arm. 'Us two will stop the Sicklies before they get away with the **GLOB** piece.'

'Be careful, Max!' said Gloop, but Max was already on the move. He lowered his head and *RACED* straight for the closest Gool—a bright pink one with creepy yellow eyes. Just before he hit it, he threw himself to the  ground and slid in a patch of **pixel slime**.

Keeping his head low, Max *SKIDDED* along underneath the ghosts, then *JUMPED* to his feet when he reached the other side.

An orange Gool made a grab for him, but a ball of hardened **slime THONKED** off the back of its head. Captain Crust stared down the barrel of his gun-cane and gave a satisfied nod. '**GOTCHA!**' he said. The Gool broke up into lots of **little orange pixels**, which then fell to the floor like dust. A moment later, the Gool's eyes landed on top of the pile and sat there, blinking in surprise.

'Now go, Max!' Captain Crust urged. 'Get that piece of **GOLDEN GLOB**!'

Max *CHARGED* out of the maze and frantically looked around. The Bogey Bus was right where they'd left it, but there was no sign of the Sicklies anywhere.

# ATCHOO!

'That way,' sniffed Atishoo, nodding towards the opening that led out onto the mountainside track. 'They've gone outside!'

Max *RAN*. If Bubble Kitten got away she could hide anywhere in the volcano. They might never find her—or the **GLOB** piece—again.

The sun was **BLINDING** as Max, cradling the tiny Goozilla in his hand, *RACED* out through the hole in the volcano wall.

'S-stop!' Atishoo squeaked, and Max skidded to a stop right at the edge of the cliff. Far below, he could see the **bubbling gloop** that surrounded the volcano's base.

'**AH, THERE YOU ARE!**' said a sneering voice that Max recognized all too well. He turned, then felt his blood run cold. Bubble Kitten, Sugar Paws, and Glitter Chick stood a little way down the track and between them and Max were lots of colourful eggs, all spread out across the ground.

'**ALRIGHT?**' grunted Glitter Chick.

'I wouldn't move if I were you,' warned Bubble Kitten. 'One wrong step and you'll both go kablooey!'

She waved the piece of the **GOLDEN GLOB** around, teasing them. 'And you came so close to getting this back. Such a shame.'

A rip-roaring **sneeze ERUPTED** from
Atishoo and he *FIRED* through the air like
a missile. Bubble Kitten's face fell as she
realized what was about to happen.

'Oh dear,' she sighed.

# ING!

Atishoo hit Bubble Kitten right between the eyes, then bounced back. Max grabbed for the little Goozilla, catching him before he went *SHOOTING* right over the cliff edge.

'THANKS, MAX!'

Atishoo beamed.

'It doesn't matter!' said Bubble Kitten, rubbing her forehead. Sugar Paws tried to lend her a paw, but she batted it away in annoyance. **'GET OFF, YOU STUPID MUTT!'**

She straightened up and attempted to look impressive. 'As I was saying . . . it doesn't matter because I still have this,' she said, holding out a paw.

An empty paw.

'**WHAT?**' she muttered, confusion clouding her pretty pink face. 'Where's the **GLOB**?'

From inside Atishoo there came a

**GOLDEN GLOW**. Max could just make out the outline of the **GLOB** piece inside the little Goozilla's belly. 'Looks like you lost again, Bubble Kitten!' Max laughed. Atishoo's face crinkled up and Max braced himself. 'And looks like Atishoo's got a **GLOB**-powered **supersneeze** brewing.'

AAAAA...

AAAAAAA...

Atishoo's sneeze BOOMED like thunder. Bubble Kitten, Sugar Paws, and Glitter Chick all hugged each other and howled in fright as Glitter Chick's explosive eggs were blasted towards them by the force of the mighty sneeze.

KABO

# OM!

The eggs **ERUPTED** in a deafening explosion of smoke and glitter.

Max and Atishoo watched as the Sicklies went tumbling down towards the ocean of goo far below.

**'I'LL GET YOU FOR THIIIIIIIS!'** Bubble Kitten wailed, then she frantically tried to blow a bubble that would carry them to safety.

'Sorry!' Atishoo called after the falling Sicklies. 'Allergic to feathers.'

Max laughed. 'And I, for one, am *really* glad you are!'

# CHAPTER TEN

# HOMEWARD BOUND

When Max and Atishoo returned to the maze, they found the rest of the Goozillas standing around several **piles of pixels**. A set of eyeballs blinked on top of each pile.

'You defeated the Gools!' cried Max.

'Did you get the **GLOB** piece?' asked Gloop.

'We did! Well, actually, it was all Atishoo,' Max said. The little Goozilla was sitting on his shoulder, and blushed a darker shade of green when everyone turned his way.

'Aw,' he said. 'It was nothing.'

'Two pieces of the **GLOB** collected, four to go,' said Gunk.

Captain Crust pulled down his hat and twitched his moustache. 'Then what are we waiting for? Let's go and find the next . . .'

**BEEP-BEEP-BEEP!**

Max groaned. It was his screen time alarm. His time in the game was up. 'I have to go,' he said, sadly.

His legs started to w**o**bble and he felt like the volcano was about to flip itself upside-down. 'But I'll be back soon! I promise!'

Captain Crust snapped off a salute. 'We'll be ready and waiting!'

'See you soon, Max!' said Gloop.

'Thanks for all your—'

But Max didn't hear the end of Joe's

sentence. Instead, he heard the **THUDDING** of footsteps on the stairs as he arrived back in his room, just as Amy burst in with a box of tissues.

'Here,' she said, tossing the box onto the bed and grabbing for the tablet. 'Mum says to come down for breakfast, and that you have to give me the tablet *right now*!'

Max shrugged. Now his screen time had run out, he couldn't play **WORLD OF SLIME** anyway. 'Go for it,' he said, and he watched over Amy's shoulder as she logged in and tapped the World of Pets icon.

As soon as the app loaded, she **GASPED**, and Max had to bite his lip to stop himself laughing because there, on the screen, was

Bubble Kitten. Her pink fur was standing on end, and she was covered head to toe in shimmery sparkles and blobs of bright green gloop.

'WOW!' exclaimed Amy. 'What happened to Bubble Kitten?'

'I don't know,' said Max, hiding his grin behind a tissue. 'It looks like she's been

in an **EGGS-PLOSION**. You'd better take **EGGS-TRA** good care of her.'

As his sister left the room, Max lay back on his bed. His second visit to the **WORLD OF SLIME** had been even more exciting than the first.

He couldn't wait to find out what adventure he and his Goozilla friends would end up in tomorrow.